10 Minute Classics

Good books are some of the greatest treasures in the world. They can take you to incredible places and on fantastic adventures. So sit back with a 10 MINUTE CLASSIC and indulge a lifelong love for reading.

We cannot, however, guarantee your 10 minute break won't turn into 15, 20, or 30 minutes, as these FUN stories and engaging pictures will have you turning the pages AGAIN and AGAIN!

Designed by Flowerpot Press
in Franklin, TN.
www.FlowerpotPress.com
Designer: Stephanie Meyers
Editor: Johannah Gilman Paiva
DJS-0912-0142
ISBN: 978-1-4867-0861-1
Made in China/Fabriqué en Chine

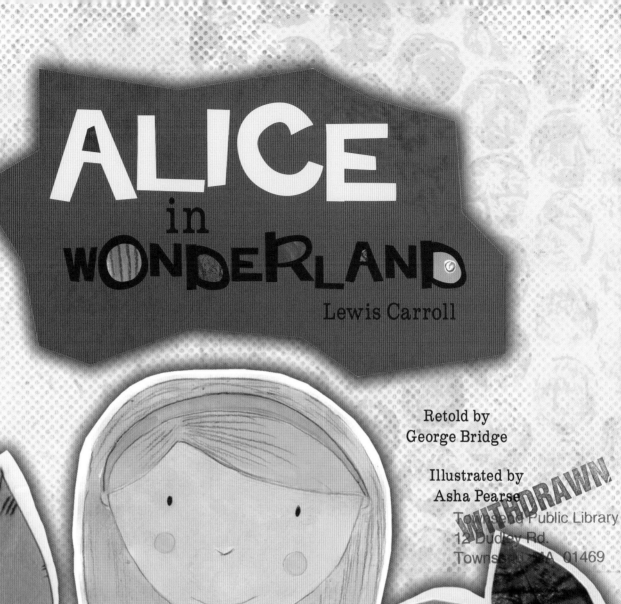

ALICE
in
WONDERLAND

Lewis Carroll

Retold by
George Bridge

Illustrated by
Asha Pearse

This is the story of a little girl named Alice, who lived not too long ago in a place not too far from here. Alice loved books, adored adventures, and found herself to be very curious about a great many things. Alice had some amazing adventures in a place called Wonderland...

"I'm late! I'm late!"

One day, Alice was resting by a river with her sister when a rabbit ran past. This was not just an everyday rabbit—this was a white rabbit dressed in fine clothes and carrying a pocket watch.

Alice watched as the White Rabbit hurried into a rabbit hole and disappeared from sight. Being curious, she quickly followed. And then she fell...

and fell...

and fell...

for what seemed like a very long time, indeed!

Alice eventually landed in a room with many locked doors. These were the doors to Wonderland! Behind one very small locked door, Alice could see a lovely garden, but she was too big to fit through the door. It made Alice feel very sad, indeed, to be stuck in a rabbit hole, too big to crawl out.

Just then, Alice noticed a little
table with delightful refreshments,
just waiting to be tried.

First, she tried drinking a potion marked,
"Drink me," but it made her too small.

Then, she tried eating some cake marked,
"Eat me," but it made her too big.

eat me

Drink me

That's when Alice began to cry...

and cry...

and cry...

for what seemed like quite a long time, indeed.

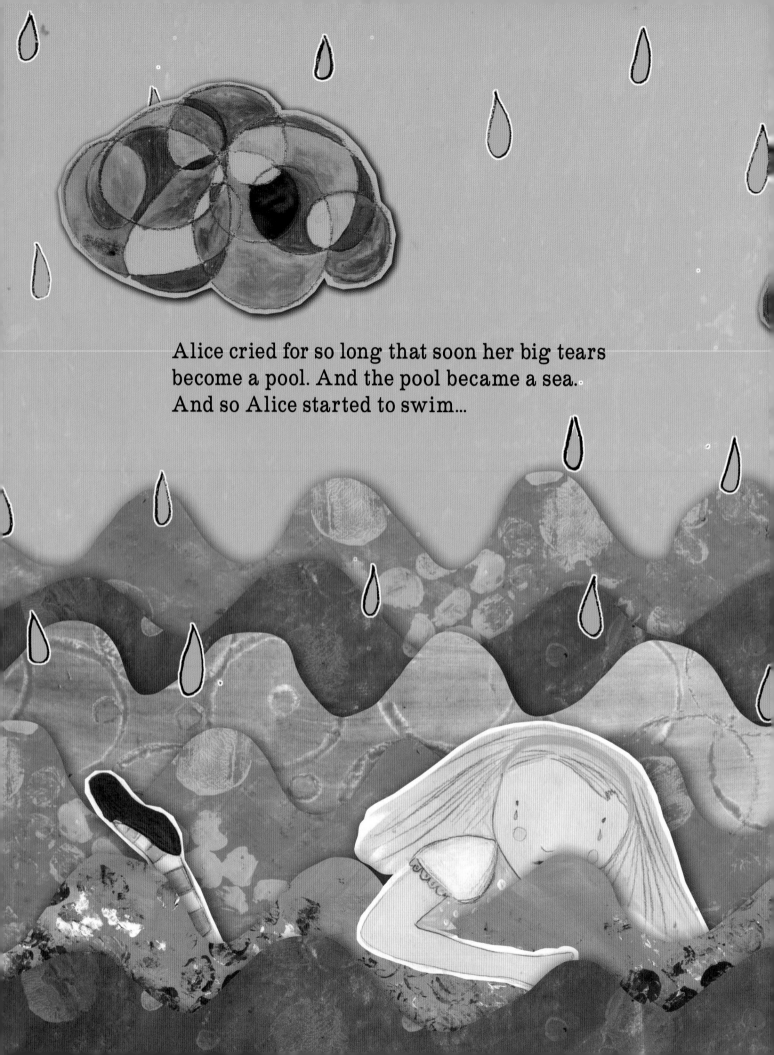

Alice cried for so long that soon her big tears become a pool. And the pool became a sea. And so Alice started to swim...

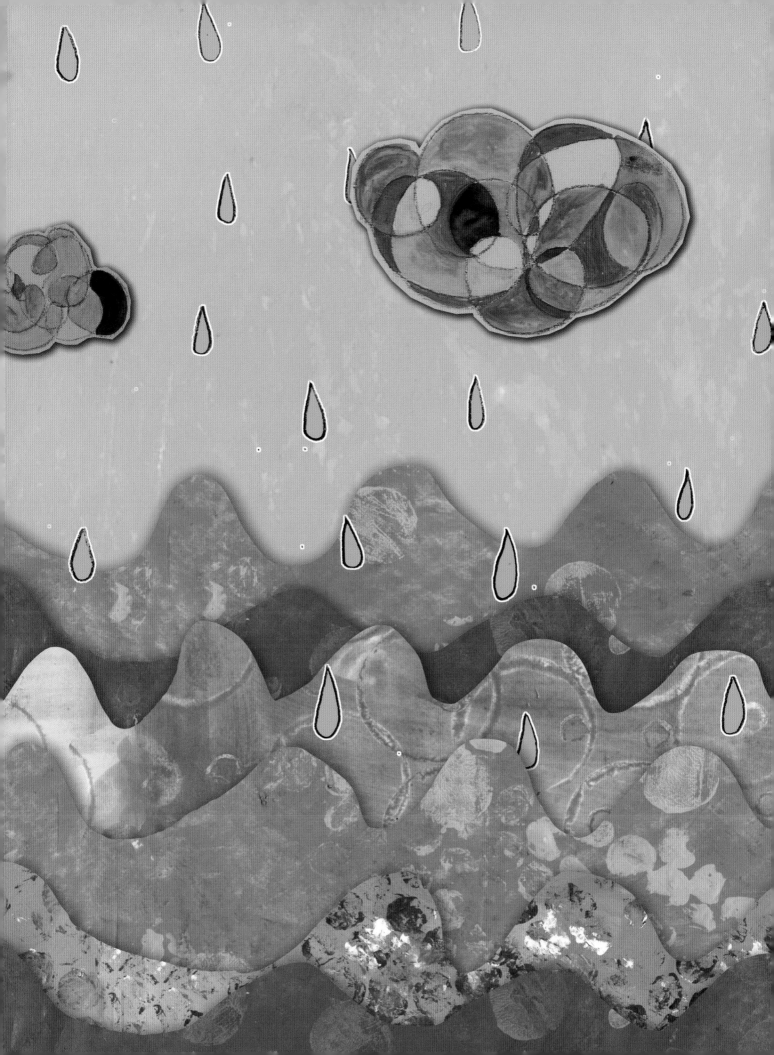

As Alice was swimming for shore, she met a mouse, and then a number of other animals, and when they all got to shore, they were wet. To dry themselves off, the friends listened to a very dry lecture by the mouse. Then, they raced in a circle, but it didn't go anywhere.

Alice had never talked to animals before, except her cat, Dinah, so she told her new animal friends stories about Dinah. Stories of a cat only scared them away.

Once again, Alice was alone.

It can feel scary to be alone in a strange place. Alice felt a bit scared, but she also felt very curious, so she stood up, brushed herself off, and began to wander through Wonderland. There she met many interesting characters, and had many curious adventures...

Alice saw the White Rabbit again, who treated her like a servant.

He demanded Alice find his mislaid fan and gloves, so she made her way to his house to find them, thinking all the while how odd it was to take orders from a rabbit.

Next on her adventure, Alice met a caterpillar resting on top of a giant mushroom. "Who are you?" the caterpillar asked her. While Alice tried to explain who she was, the caterpillar argued with her, which made Alice feel a bit cross.

Then, Alice met the Duchess, who went off to play croquet with the Queen of Hearts. Alice tried to ask the Duchess a question, but instead of answering helpfully, the Duchess insulted her for not knowing the answer.

Alice kept walking, and met a grinning Cheshire Cat, who explained to Alice that everyone in Wonderland was mad,* including her.

Following directions from the Cheshire Cat, Alice found her way to the March Hare's house, where she joined a most peculiar tea party...

*In this circumstance, "mad" means a little bit crazy, rather than angry.

Sitting at a huge table, sipping tea and talking nonsense, were the March Hare and the Mad Hatter. Between them was the Dormouse, who was asleep. They decided to put their sleepy friend in the teapot.

Immediately, the Mad Hatter and the March Hare bombarded Alice with riddles and gibberish. In answer to one of their many questions, Alice responded in confusion, "I don't think..."

But, before she could finish, the Mad Hatter interrupted, "Then you shouldn't talk!"

This bit of rudeness was more than Alice could bear. She walked off in disgust.

Nobody seemed to notice.

Alice eventually found her way to a garden ruled by the Queen of Hearts and filled with curious characters. Together, they all played croquet...

"Off with his head!" shouted the Queen at just about everything and everyone she didn't like. This soon led to a trial, which led to a dispute between Alice and the Queen of Hearts.

"Off with her head!" shouted the Queen at Alice, but Alice was unafraid.

"You're all just a pack of cards!" Alice shouted to the Queen's guards. That's when the cards started to swarm all over her...

Alice was furiously swiping away the attacking cards when she heard a familiar voice...

"Alice! Wake up!" shouted her sister.

Alice woke up. She was back by the river. As she sat up, she finished brushing away the leaves that had landed on her while she was sleeping.

And she thought, "That was a very strange sleep, indeed."